HUGGING GRANDMA

By Zina Kramer

Illustrations by
Dave Messing

Loving Those
with Memory
Disorders

Ferne Press

Hugging Grandma
Loving Those with Memory Disorders

Copyright © 2009 by Zina Kramer
Illustrated by Dave Messing
Printed in Canada

Summary: A little girl finds positive ways to help her grandmother who has Alzheimer's disease.

Library of Congress Cataloging-in-Publication Data
Kramer, Zina
Hugging Grandma: Loving Those with Memory Disorders / Zina Kramer – First Edition
ISBN-13: 978-1-933916-38-5
1. Alzheimer's Disease 2. Dementia 3. Memory Disorder 4. Children 5. Dignity 6. Compassion
I. Kramer, Zina II. Hugging Grandma: Loving Those with Memory Disorders
Library of Congress Control Number: 2009921396

FERNE PRESS

Ferne Press is an imprint of Nelson Publishing & Marketing
366 Welch Road, Northville, MI 48167
www.nelsonpublishingandmarketing

This book is dedicated with love to my mother,
Sylvia Perlman, who always remembered
the positive side of life. She remains my
greatest inspiration.

Acknowledgments

I want to give a special thank you to my husband, Michael; my children, Lisa and David; my daughter-in-law, Anessa; my sister, Anita; my brother-in-law, Ralph; and my nephew, Bradley, for creating a network of love and support for Grandma Sylvia. Everyone took the time to return to Grandma Sylvia the great love and life lessons that she provided for each of us. Sam, her first great-grandson, provided her with some of the smiles we all thought she had lost.

And a huge thank you goes to the Alzheimer's Association for helping us to better understand my mother's new life.

I want to extend my sincere gratitude to the loving staff of the Dorothy & Peter Brown Jewish Community Adult Day Care Program for continuing to provide love and patience, along with enjoyable activities, during Grandma Sylvia's declining years. The staff provided patience during the day, which enabled me to have patience during the portion of the day when Grandma Sylvia resided with us. The Brown Program helped engage Grandma Sylvia in her life's work—loving people.

And I can't forget a special tribute to the wonderful angels, Ruthie, Odella, and Wanda, who treated my mother with dignity in her later stages.

Last, but not least, it was my father, Harold, who always emphasized the importance of continuous learning to enhance life's experiences.

A portion of the proceeds will benefit the Dorothy & Peter Brown Jewish Community Adult Day Care Program and the Alzheimer's Association

My favorite thing to do with Grandma Sylvia is to play Store.
She takes cans and boxes filled with real food from
her kitchen and puts them in a brown paper bag.

Then we go out to her backyard,
and I sell things to her and she buys them.

Sometimes I stop to pat her hair or touch the shiny gold charms that look like children hanging from her gold necklace. She always wears pretty gold bracelets too.

Her arms are wrinkled and shiny. I asked her
once if they were covered in plastic wrap.
She laughed and gave me a squeeze.

Grandma giggles at the silly things I say.
When she laughs, her eyes twinkle and her body shakes.

Every time I visit my grandma, she hugs me as soon
as I get in the door. She always has lots of time
just for me. She makes me feel so special.

Everything tastes really yummy in Grandma's kitchen.
She always smells like the food she is cooking.

Sometimes, when I am ready for lunch, she says,
"Do you want some vegetable soup? I'll put hot dogs in it,
so it will taste better." She makes the best soup ever.
No one else but Grandma puts hot dogs in my soup.

When Grandma takes me to the beach, she tells her friends all about me. She tells them how smart and pretty I am.

I love playing in the sand with my grandma. She always knows just how much water to put in my sand cakes.

I would rather be with my grandma than with anyone else in the whole world.

But now Grandma's acting different. She says the same things over and over again. I say, "Grandma, you already told me that." Then she says it again.

We don't go to the mall to buy toys or dresses anymore.
Grandma doesn't cook for me or play with me,
and she doesn't laugh like she used to.

She even forgot my birthday. I am so sad.
My mom says, "We are all sad about Grandma Sylvia."

"What's wrong with Grandma? Doesn't she love me anymore?"

"Of course Grandma loves you," Mom says.
"Grandma has a sickness that is called Alzheimer's disease.
It makes it hard for her to remember things. She's still our
Grandma Sylvia and she has filled our lives with happiness.
Now it is our turn to treat her extra special."

"How can I make Grandma feel good?" I ask Mom.

"Grandma needs lots of help because she forgets," Mom explains. "You may need to tell her your name and show her family pictures. You can tell her who everyone is. Don't worry; I will be with you to figure out all the things that you can do for Grandma now."

So now I give Grandma water when she is thirsty. And sometimes when she is hungry, I bring her some vegetable soup. I always put hot dogs in it because I know it is the best soup ever.

Instead of playing Store, I help Grandma put her groceries away. I take the towels out of the dryer for her and we fold them together. Mom says all of these things make Grandma feel "needed and helpful."

Sometimes I sing songs, play some of her favorite music, or call to tell her about my day. Mom tells me that all of these things make Grandma feel good too.

On Grandma's birthday, Mom and I made a scrapbook of all the great things she used to do with us. It helped me think about all of our special times together. Mom says she is grateful for all of the great memories that we have.

Now when I brush Grandma's hair, or pat it like I used to, or even when I help Grandma put on her necklace and gold bracelets, I think about when we used to play Store in her backyard. I love remembering those times.

"We know in our hearts that Grandma still loves us. She just has trouble saying it," Mom says.

And just like Grandma used to say, "I love you,"
now I will hold her hand, give her a hug, and say,
"Grandma, I love you."

A Note to Parents

As hard as it is for adults to know how to react to the seemingly irrational behavior of someone with Alzheimer's or dementia, it is most difficult for children. I wrote *Hugging Grandma* to explain this illness to children and help them find positive ways to cope. I hope that my book can be a catalyst for meaningful conversation within families who are affected by a memory disorder, and can help create a positive strategy for continued interaction with a loved one.

People experience Alzheimer's in so many different ways. The behaviors of those who have Alzheimer's, as well as each family's situation and reactions, are unique. This book is only based on our family's story.

Hugging Grandma was inspired by the life of my amazing mother, Sylvia Perlman. She was the lone member of her family to survive the Holocaust, and later in life became a survivor of colon and breast cancer. Through all of this, my mother always believed she was lucky; she never felt victimized. Instead, she was grateful for the blessings of life and approached life from an innately positive view.

When she was diagnosed with Alzheimer's disease and lived with our family, we learned how important it was to help her feel useful and continue to engage her in social situations. She enrolled in the Dorothy & Peter Brown Jewish Community Adult Day Care Program and received the love, care, and social interaction she desperately needed. As a family, we gained peace of mind knowing that during the daytime hours she was in a caring environment.

After Grandma Sylvia passed away, we experienced an outpouring of affection and thankfulness for her and for the wisdom that she shared. Without question, her grandchildren were enriched and more secure as a result of their grandmother's unconditional love and complete devotion.

As we, her family, sorted through her things, her life could be summarized by the sign she kept in the kitchen: "When life gives you lemons, make lemonade."

Zina Kramer

Interacting with Your Special Grandparent

Listen to music

Make homemade lemonade

Take photos together and make a collage

Look at family photos

Frost cupcakes or cookies

Put silverware away

Make a scrapbook

Fold towels

Water house plants

Walk around the yard

Sort change

Ask them about their favorite pet

Ask them about their first car

Talk about your favorite times together

Sing their favorite songs with them or to them

Cook a favorite family recipe together
(vegetable soup with hot dogs!)

Hold their hand

Give them a hug

Treat them with dignity and compassion

Explaining Alzheimer's Disease to Children

Even though someone in your family has Alzheimer's disease, you cannot catch it; and it doesn't mean that you will get it someday. Alzheimer's disease affects the brain, and it causes people to have trouble remembering and thinking. This also impairs their ability to talk and take care of themselves. Medicine can help, but it cannot cure this disease. Hopefully, someday scientists will develop a medicine that will.

For assistance in dealing with a loved one with Alzheimer's disease, go to www.alz.org or visit www.zinakramerbooks.com.

About the Author

Photo by Les Gorback

The seeds for Zina Kramer's life-long commitment to public service were planted in the wake of World War II, where she was born to two Holocaust survivors. Fleeing several European countries, she came to the United States with her parents at the age of two. She has always had a deep appreciation for her freedom and a determination to help others.

Having grown up without grandparents, Zina observed the special relationship that her parents and children shared. She learned how to be a grandma from watching her own parents with their grandchildren. Unfortunately, she also witnessed how devastating Alzheimer's can be to children. After six years of caring for her mother, an Alzheimer's patient, and having a mother-in-law with dementia, Zina wrote *Hugging Grandma*. She hopes this book provides some comfort for the great number of children affected by a loved one with a memory disorder.

Zina is a marketing executive whose emphasis is public service. She loves politics and has a special fondness for Election Day and what it represents. She lives in Michigan with her husband Michael and their dog Lexi. They have a wonderful family including David, Anessa, and Lisa, and two very adored grandchildren, Sam and Max.

About the Illustrator

David Messing is a life-long artist, illustrator, cartoonist, sculptor, writer, and instructor. For twenty-five years, Dave has taught at his family-owned business, Art 101. Dave also designs and builds props, sets, and miniatures for print and film commercials. His work can be seen on TV, billboards, in national magazines, and in movies.

Please visit www.davemessing.741.com.

When *Life* gives you **Lemons** make *Lemonade*